for Gerry,
with love,
Jeri

TOM-CAT-LION

Jeni Couzyn

illustrated by Paul Demeyer

LONDON   VICTOR GOLLANCZ LTD   1987

Tom-Cat-Lion was a fierce hunter.

He chased the squirrels
up the horse chestnut tree.

He chased the frogs
who lived under stones.

He chased the hungry blackbirds
trying to eat their dinner.

"Leave the birds alone, Tom-Cat-Lion," said Mrs Harty,
flapping her tea towel at him. But Tom-Cat-Lion growled
at her. He wasn't afraid of a tea towel!

He was the bravest hunter in Chestnut Valley.

One night it was very cold. Antonia made a curling-up space
for Tom-Cat-Lion among her teddy bears on the end of her bed.
He liked Antonia's cosy bedroom.

Later he went downstairs to keep Mrs Harty company for a while. She put his special velvet cushion on the table by the window, so he could keep an eye on the stars.

At last the moon rose.
Tom-Cat-Lion went out through his cat-flap, across the park, and up the hill.

At the top of Chestnut Hall he settled down to survey his kingdom.

"Whoo," said Owl, "you're in
for a nasty shock, Tom-Cat-Lion."
"What do you mean?" asked
Tom-Cat-Lion, but Owl swooped
away into the horse chestnuts.

The next day was Antonia's birthday. Mrs Harty had a present for her in a basket. Before Antonia even opened it, Tom-Cat-Lion knew something was wrong. The whole house smelled of wrongness.

Inside the basket was a ball of silvery fluff.
"Look, Tom-Cat-Lion," cried Antonia. "Isn't she beautiful! I shall call her Silky."

Tom-Cat-Lion
tried to eat Silky up
with one big bite, but Antonia
wouldn't let him.

"Let's play, Tom-Cat-Lion," cried Silky in her
little silvery voice. Tom-Cat-Lion growled his
deadly hunter growl, and bared his teeth,
but she wasn't frightened of him at all.

She kissed him by touching noses.

She jumped out at him from behind the bookcase.

When he was eating his dinner she bit his tail.

"Isn't she adorable?" said Mrs Harty, but Tom-Cat-Lion wouldn't answer.
He curled himself into a ball behind the coal-bucket.
"Oh, Tom-Cat-Lion," said Mrs Harty, "when are you going to stop sulking?"

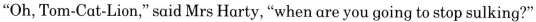

Tom-Cat-Lion's life was all spoiled.
Silky was always curled up on the lap or the mat or the cushion he wanted.
"*Silky, Silky, Silky,*" said Antonia and Mrs Harty. He wanted Silky to go away.
The wanting turned into a hard lump of sadness in his tummy.

He decided to leave home.
The cold air bit his eyes as he banged out through his cat-flap.
The freezing wind made his tail bristle, but he didn't care.

He was alone in the world.

Suddenly he felt the
shadow of Owl over him.
"I want Silky to go away,"
sighed Tom-Cat-Lion.
"Silky will not go away,"
said Owl.
"But she's making me so
sad," said Tom-Cat-Lion,
and two big tears rolled
down his nose.

"It's the *I WANT* in your tummy that's making you sad.
You must get rid of it, spit it out," said Owl.

Tom-Cat-Lion coughed

and spat

and sputtered,

but still . . .

I WANT THERE TO BE NO SILKY lay in his tummy like a stone.

"Help me, Owl," said Tom-Cat-Lion.
"All right," said Owl. "Make yourself soft.
Pretend to be asleep."

Suddenly Owl swooped down,
lifted Tom-Cat-Lion by his tail
and flew him up over the treetops,
over the domes of Chestnut Hall . . .

up and up towards the moon.

At the highest point in the sky ... "Now," shouted Owl, "open
your eyes!" Tom-Cat-Lion peeped out through one eye just as Owl
opened his claws and let him go. As he plunged towards the ground,
he saw Silky, tiny as a grass-seed among the lights of the city.
It made him smile.

With a hot whistling sound his lump of wanting flew
out of his mouth and disappeared into the dark.

25

And then Owl had him again, firmly grasped in his strong claws as he drifted gently back to earth.

Tom-Cat-Lion was lying quite still on the frozen ground.
When he uncurled himself and looked around, Owl had gone,
and the sun was just beginning to rise over the edge of the hill.
But he felt different. With his lump of wanting gone,
he felt as still and bright inside as the wintry dawn.

"I am Tom-Cat-Lion," he said to himself. "I am a brave hunter. I live in Chestnut Valley, with my little girl Antonia and comfortable Mrs Harty and gentle little Silky. I think I'll go home now."

28

When Silky heard the cat-flap bang, she ran to meet him,
and he put out his nose for her to kiss.

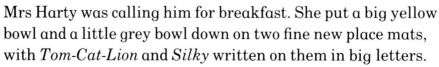

Mrs Harty was calling him for breakfast. She put a big yellow bowl and a little grey bowl down on two fine new place mats, with *Tom-Cat-Lion* and *Silky* written on them in big letters.

After breakfast Tom-Cat-Lion went upstairs to see
if Antonia was awake yet. She had moved all her
teddy bears on to her toy box, so there was room for
two cats at the bottom of her bed, one on each foot.

First published in Great Britain 1987
by Victor Gollancz Ltd
14 Henrietta Street, London WC2E 8QJ

Text © Jeni Couzyn 1987
Illustrations © Paul Demeyer 1987

British Library Cataloguing in Publication Data
Couzyn, Jeni
Tom-cat-lion.
I. Title II. Demeyer, Paul
813' .54 [J] PZ7

ISBN 0-575-04145-5

Printed in Hong Kong by Imago Publishing Limited